About the Author

John Prince is the father of one son. He is a college student with an associate in health science, working on his bachelor's degree with high ambitions of furthering his education in the medical field. John loves to spend his free time writing poems and other projects. John loves to intrigue and relax the minds of people by providing a stimulating book to cozy up to.

Blood of The Last True Heart

John Prince

Blood of The Last True Heart

Olympia Publishers
London

www.olympiapublishers.com
OLYMPIA PAPERBACK EDITION

Copyright © John Prince 2023

The right of John Prince to be identified as author of
this work has been asserted in accordance with sections 77 and 78 of
the Copyright, Designs and Patents Act 1988.

All Rights Reserved

No reproduction, copy or transmission of this publication
may be made without written permission.
No paragraph of this publication may be reproduced,
copied or transmitted save with the written permission of the publisher,
or in accordance with the provisions
of the Copyright Act 1956 (as amended).

Any person who commits any unauthorised act in relation to
this publication may be liable to criminal
prosecution and civil claims for damage.

A CIP catalogue record for this title is
available from the British Library.

ISBN: 978-1-80439-240-9

This is a work of fiction.
Names, characters, places and incidents originate from the writer's
imagination. Any resemblance to actual persons, living or dead, is
purely coincidental.

First Published in 2023

Olympia Publishers
Tallis House
2 Tallis Street
London
EC4Y 0AB

Printed in Great Britain

Dedication

I dedicate this book to my mother, Malarian.

Acknowledgements

Special thanks to my friends, family, and cat, for letting me be me. Also, a big thanks for my late dog Cai! To all, I love you!

When you arise in the morning, think of what a privilege it is to be alive, to think, to enjoy, and to love.
– Marcus Aurelius

In Peace

My name is Samantha, but I prefer the name Sam. It's shorter and matches my tomboyish personality. I was born and raised in what used to be a quiet little town east of Kansas. I lived with my mom and dad – Curie and Joe – my older brother, Jake, younger brother, Timothy, and my best friend in the world. Not to forget my pet chicken, Matthew! The only thing is that I had to keep her a secret. My dad didn't like having farm animals as pets. Yeah, I was raised on a farm. Corn, cows, chickens, the whole nine yards. More like 244 acres. All the chickens were great, though no chicken quite like my Matthew. Her big, fluffy, black feathers. When the sun pierced those feathers, I could see a hint of blue on the tips of them. I loved her so much. Yeah, he was a she; it's complicated, but you'll see why later. Well, I'm twenty-nine now. Things have gotten, well, pretty freaking complicated. The blood of the true heart is still running through my veins, and I'm a vegan now, but now it's pretty much required to survive. The sky's a dark red now, with clouds like blood clots.

Almost all the rivers and streams that were once a crisp pristine blue now run a dark, bloody red. The world wasn't always like this.

Sometimes it's hard to remember how things used to be. I guess I would have to take you back a decade. All the way back to when I was a teenager in high school on my parent's' farm.

Chapter 1

Chicken Little

"Cock-a-doodle-doo!"
　　The rooster crows every day before sunrise, letting my family know it's time to get the day started. Of course, I'm already awake; I wake up extra early to spend time with Matthew. "Matthew, how are you today?" The chicken stares as it ruffles its beautiful black feathers. "You're the best, Matthew."
　　"Sam, are you out here?" my father cries.
　　"I'm right here, Dad."
　　"What are you doing out here so early?"
　　"I... I just wanted to get an early start on my chores."
　　"That's great, Sam, but your mother is setting the table. Let's go eat, then you can get ready for school."
　　"Bye, Matthew, I'll see you after school,"

　　'I whisper to my pet chicken as I quickly run to catch up with my father.
　　"Good morning, Mom!"
　　"Good morning, Samantha."
　　I squint my face.
　　"Mom, it's Sam," Jake laughs. "Why don't you just change your name to 'hi, I'm single'," he says.
　　"Mom!" I scream.

"Jake, don't tease your sister."

"I'm just saying, Mom, bad enough she dresses like a boy, and plays in the dirt like a boy. Now, she wants to be called Sam, too."

Joe walks into the kitchen. "Jake, that's enough, now walk your sister and little brother to the bus stop."

"Okay, Dad," Jake says as gets up to walk with me.

"Timothy, Sam, I want you guys to come straight home for supper, all right? So that means I don't want you to miss the bus, and Jake, I wanna see your face at the table too. Your mother and I work too hard to see empty seats at the table," says Joe.

All three of us kids sigh. "Okay."

The bus tires screech.

"All right, hop on." The bus driver says in a blasé tone. Timothy and I hop on the bus as Jake drove off, taking his usual path to college. I see my friend Susie instantly. We've known each other since middle school. We hang out at school a lot but never outside of the school because she stays in the city, which is too far to drive. Oddly enough, we have a better school district here, so her parents use our address to take her to the closest drop-off point for the school bus. "Hey, Sam, come sit by me," Susie says. "Did you finish your math assignment for Ms. Ennis' class?"

"Oh shoot," I gasp, "I totally forgot. I was so busy playing with Matthew."

"That chicken!" screams Susie.

"Yes..." I whisper, "and could you keep your voice down, everybody already thinks I'm weird enough," I say in embarrassment.

Susie growls, "Yeah, that was happening before you

started talking to chickens, ha ha!"

"Shut up, Susie!"

The bus stops.

"All right, kids, get!" the bus driver howls at the students. My face cringes at the bus driver as I think, You know, I can walk to school.

We get off the bus and approach Jimmy Water High.

"The weirdest part is that you named that chicken after your crush, Matt," Susie says.

I blush immediately. "He's not my–"

Susie stares.

"Okay, maybe I have a little crush on him."

"Umm... ya, you think?"

The bell rings. "Oh, darn," I say, "see you at lunch period, Susie."

"Okay, later. Oh, and good luck in Ms. Ennis' class!" says Susie.

"Ms. Ennis!" I shout. "Oh, no! Not only did I not finish the assignment, I'm late!" I say with an urgent tone as I take off running, almost dislocating my shoulder while turning a corner too sharply. I approach the classroom door. Locked, I knock hesitantly. "Ms. Ennis, it's Sam."

Ms. Ennis walks over to unlock the door. "You're late; please take your seat in the front of the class," says Ms. Ennis.

"Yes, ma'am," I reply. Ms. Ennis goes on to start her class.

"All right, now that your five-minute warm-up is done, please pass forward your assignment from last night." A shiver runs deep down my spine. Because I know I didn't do it.

"Here you go, Sam." That voice sends another shiver down my spine so cold and yet warm. I cringe because that voice coming from that one boy at this time is everything to me. Well, at least in my head he is.

"Thank you, M-Ma-Matt," I say.

"I notice your dad has bought some land from my family," says Matt.

"Yeah," I say shyly.

"Well, that means we might be seeing more of each other."

"I- I can't wait!" I say awkwardly.

"Please be quiet in my classroom," Ms. Ennis yells. "Oh, and I noticed, Sam, that your assignment is not with the other students'."

"I'm sorry, Ms. Ennis, but I was so busy with my father helping out on the farm yesterday that I didn't get a chance to actually work on it."

Ms. Ennis immediately lashes out in a chaotic, borderline-violent rant. "I don't care how many chickens, goats, pigs or horses you have to tend to! When I issue an assignment, I expect it to be done. Furthermore–"

Riinnnnnng! The school bell rings.

"Okay, class, I want a review on chapters two and three, study, study, study, because we're going to have a quiz on Monday." The whole class rushes out the door like a pack of rabid dogs.

"Sam!"

"Yes, Ms. Ennis?"

"You mustn't think fat meat is greasy. Do you?"

"I'm not sure I understand, ma'am."

"The assignment was a big part of your grade, and

unless you want to end up working on your family's farm forever, you need to be more serious about this work. You're almost a high school graduate, after another year, and this is the time you need to spend reflecting on what and who you want to be when you grow up. Now, go to lunch!"

"Yes, Ms. Ennis," I reply.

I drag my feet as I walk to the cafeteria.

"Damn, Sam, what took you so long? I've been sitting here forever," Susie says as she waits impatiently eating a slice of pizza as if it was the last one left on Earth.

"I know, Susie, I'm sorry," I say. "I had to stay after class to talk to Ms. Ennis."

"Did she give you the old who-and-what-you-want-to-be-when-you-grow-up?"

"Yeah, that and a lot more! I told her I was helping my family on a farm, and she still dug into me. Imagine if she knew I didn't get the work done because I was playing with my pet chicken, Matthew."

Susie smiles. "Yeah, she would have literally roasted you alive. Speaking of being roasted alive, aren't you afraid that your family is going to eat your little friend Matthew?"

"No, we need her to lay the eggs."

"Her?" says Susie with a confused look on her face. "So let me get this straight. You're friends with a 'pet' chicken you named after a boy you have a crush on in school, and this 'chicken' is a hen?"

"Shhhhhhh," I whimper with embarrassment, "chicken is a broad term for the bird, whether it be a male or female, and, yes, besides, I don't really have any friends, and you stay in the city. She wasn't always called Matthew; she used to be called Josh, my seventh-grade crush. Well, that's at *least until his family moved to the city."*

Susie stares at me. *"Sam, you should really get out more, and I mean a lot more."*

I giggle as I glance over to see a group approaching. *"Hey, Sam, hey, Susie," Gina says.*

"Hey, Gina."

"What's up, Sam?" replied cheerfully. Gina goes on to explain.

"Well, if you don't know, I'm with the animal rights activist group, or 'A.R.A.G'. Our group believes in the protection of all animals, trees and the preservation of nature itself. We are all one and should look out for each other."

"Pfff," Susie scoffs, unbothered by Gina's emotional plea.

"So, we're going to walk around hugging trees and being afraid to eat meat," says Susie. "We all have a right to be on this planet, and if there's a way for us to naturally get the nutrients in essentials we need without harming animals or nature, we should explore that opportunity," Gina explains.

"Yeah, after school I was on my way to explore Big Belly Burger to, guess what, get a burger, so I think I'm going to pass," Susie says sarcastically.

Gina stands there looking puzzled and generally concerned for Susie. "Um, okay, what about you, Sam, are you interested in joining our group?"

"It sounds like a wonderful idea, but I just don't think I'll have time right now."

"Okay, well, if you guys change your mind you know where to find us. See you guys later," Gina says as she walks

to another table of people to discuss the group. Susie glances over to see me looking mildly interested. "You're not thinking of actually joining those tree-hugging hippies, are you, Sam?"

"Well, I think what they're doing is actually pretty cool, but with me living and working on a farm I mean it's already hard enough for me. Also, my dad wants me home and at the table by supper. Oh, you should come over, Susie!"

"Sure, it's funny I have never been to your home, sounds fun."

"It will be," I say. "I'll call and ask my dad if you can spend the night before I head back to class, so ask your folks too, Susie."

"Will Jake be there?" Susie says, blushing.

"Susie! Ew, gross, that's my brother!"

"What, he's, like, super cute."

"Okay, he's also my brother, and he's in college!" I stare at Susie with my eyes squinting. "Anyway, meet me at the hangout spot after school. I don't want to miss the bus. Plus, I have to walk a block or two to get my little brother Timothy from Elementary School."

"Wow, I keep forgetting you have a little brother," says Susie. "Is Timothy still not talking to people?"

"No, my mom says he has a condition called autism, which is why he doesn't speak, but I'll see you after school, okay?"

"Okay, Sam, see you later."

The last bell rings and the kids rush out like a flood from a broken dam. I rush over quickly to pick my little brother up from school to ensure I don't miss the bus to take us home. Timothy is standing alone, patiently waiting.

"Hey, Timothy, over here! Let's go," I yell. Timothy runs over to meet me. "I don't want to miss the bus, so we're gonna have to run a little bit," I say. "By the way, how was school?"

Timothy twitches his nose and stares blankly into the distance.

"Sam, hurry up, the driver is about to go!" Susie screams.

"All right, Timothy, let's go, we're almost there." Timothy, running as fast as he could, almost loses his footing as he glances up at a scintillating bright, red light he's seeing in the sky, followed by an even brighter white light. The white light vanishes just as quickly as it appears. The red light slowly begins to fade away. Timothy and I approach the school bus, board it and take our seats. Timothy looks visibly disturbed, unsure of what he has seen. This gauche behavior is normal for Timothy, so I pay him no mind. I turn to Susie. "It's nice that your parents let you come over to spend the night."

"Yeah, I'm really excited!" As the bus approaches the farm, Susie gasps. "Wow, so this is the farm, Sam?"

"Yeah, pretty cool huh?"

"It sure is," replies Susie.

"Come on," I say, "let me show you my room while my mom sets up the dinner table." Timothy goes into the living room as Susie and I rush up to my room. "All right, this is my room, Susie, what do you think?"

"Wow, it's a lot more girly than I expected, and it's the only room in the house that's pink."

"Well, yeah, what did you expect? A bed made out of yarn, and a deer head mounted on the wall? I mean, I'm *still a girl, you know."* Susie marvels at my room.

"I see, this is really cool," says Susie.

"Thanks, my dad helped me paint it, and my mom helped with all the floral decorations you see before you."

"With all the floral decorations you see before you," Susie mumbles in' jealousy.

"Jealous much?" I say. We stare at each other before bursting into laughter. We then both hear a loud rumble pulling into the driveway. "That must be my dad," I say. "My mom should be calling us down soon. So, you'll get a chance to meet the family."

"Okay, everybody, your dad's home. Come down for supper, come down and eat," my 'mother, Curie, yells out.

"Okay, let's go eat, Susie, then we could sneak out after dinner, and I could show you Matthew." We rush to the dinner table. There waiting already was Timothy, my' mom and my dad.

"It's very nice to finally meet you, Susie," says Mom. "Sam doesn't have many friends. In fact, you're the first one."

"Mom!" I yell.

Susie snickers.

Dad looks at me. "Have you seen your brother, Jake?"

"No, Dad, not since this morning."

"Well, he's gonna be in a world of trouble when he gets here." Dad sighs. "I don't want the food to get cold. Let's eat!"

Dad looks at Timothy. "I'm gonna make him do everybody's chores, ain't that right, Timothy?"

Timothy twitches his nose and smirks a little. My' mother then sharply turns her head toward me. "So, did anything interesting happen at school today?" she says.

"Umm no, not really, same ole thing," I nervously reply.

"Well, interestingly enough, I got a phone call from Ms. Ennis today. She said you missed an assignment for her class, and insisted that we lower your chores on the farm to keep you from missing any more of her homework."

"She said all that, huh?" I reply.

"She also said Sam doesn't think fat meat is greasy, and I told her, well, of course it is." Everybody burst into laughter except for Susie.

"It's a farm joke," I say.

"Oh, ha... ha..." Susie chuckles nervously. "Speaking of," Susie says, "this fried chicken is absolutely delicious."

"Thank you, and it should be," says Dad. "It's one of our healthiest and juiciest chickens; the mother hen."

Those words echo through my' head. My face grows pale, and my expression is cold and morbid. "Wh–what did you say?" I say.

"You know the mother hen, Sam, she's been there since you were about yay high." His hand is placed to his waist, four feet off the ground. As my father speaks, my expression grows more and more repugnant. I catch a chill and start to sweat, suddenly making a mad dash for the bathroom upstairs. As I rush to the bathroom, Susie squints her eyes because she thinks she sees glowing, blue veins on her forearm, but she is only moving too fast.

Several toilet flushes later, I hears a knock on the door. It's Mom. "Sam, are you okay?" she says.

"Why did you have to cook the mother hen? Why!"

I look at my mother, still sweating.

"We always cook the chickens and eat them, Sam, you know that."

"Yeah, but this one was in our family for years. She was my friend." My mother looks worried.

"I'm sorry, Sam, I never thought about that. That's why we don't name the animals on the farm, because we eat them."

I gag. "Well I won't have to worry about that, because I'm never eating meat again!"

Chapter 2

Vegan?

Later on that night, I lay in my bed. Susie stretches out her legs as she lies comfortably on a pallet she made on the floor, both eyes wide open, stunned at what happened earlier at dinner. "I'm sorry about what happened earlier, Sam," Susie says, "but are you really going vegan? How can you ever expect me to eat another piece of meat ever?"

My face draws a blank expression as I talk to Susie with my fingers grasping my stomach. "I still feel so sick to my stomach every time I think about it. I know it may seem crazy, but Matthew was like a dog or a cat. I know it was just a freaking chicken, but for years she's been here. Sometimes I feel like it's only me on this farm. Sure, I have my family, but my brother's always off doing his thing and my mom really likes to take care of the house. I do like to spend time with my dad, but he works often, and you know the case with Timothy. So, when I feel lonely, I've been able to just go talk, and it felt like she was listening to me. That's what made our connection so special to me."

Susie looks concerned for her friend. "I guess I understand, Sam. It's been a long day. Let's just get some sleep and we can talk about it in the morning."

When the morning comes, Susie wakes to see an empty bed where I was laying. Being in someone else's home, she is cautious to go look for me, but just as she is about to stand up, I come through the door. "Good morning, Susie!" I say enthusiastically.

"Um, good morning, Sam. You seem awfully cheery today."

"That's because I am," I say with a creepy grin stretched across my face from cheek to cheek. "I'm still sad about what happened last night, but I figured out what I can do that might help me become a vegan."

"Which is?"

"Well, do you remember what Gina was talking about at lunch yesterday?"

"Yeah, of course, the whole save-the-world monkey-plant crap," Susie says mockingly. "Sam, listen to me, I know you had a horrible experience, and I would be really sad too if I just ate my best friend, but that doesn't mean you have to change your whole life. This whole vegan thing, I mean, it's a crazy idea. They have all these people roaming around trying to eat leaves and grass. I mean, people have been eating meat, hunting animals and using bark for firewood for as long as humanity has been around, and we seem to be doing just fine."

"I think it's a little bit deeper than that, Susie," I say, "and besides, I owe it to Mathew. I simply couldn't stomach another piece of meat in my mouth ever again."

Susie looks visibly frustrated. "Yeah, and I'm sure if your crush Matt was here, you'll be singing a different tune," Susie says.

I turn bright red. "Oh my gosh, Susie, shut up!"

"I'm just saying."

"Yeah, imma need you to say less, a lot less," I say with

a grin on my face, blushing harder.

We stop laughing to a knock on the door – it's my mom.

"Sam, your brother didn't come home for dinner last night and he still isn't in his room this morning, have you heard anything from him?"

"No, Mom, he probably just decided to stay at his girlfriend's house."

"Well, I called her, and she hasn't seen him today or Friday at school, either."

"That's weird and not like him," I say. "What are we going to do, Mom?"

"Your father is down at the police station right now making a report. I just hope they come walking through that door any minute now. In the meantime, Timothy is eating breakfast. If you girls are hungry, you should go and join him..."

"Okay, Mom, let's go, Susie."

At the table, Timothy sits quietly, and we sit quietly also, with a puzzled look on our faces. My Mom washes the dishes and cleans up. Humming tunes and grinning, but you can feel the anxiety and worry flowing from her. I hear a horn blow in the driveway. "That's my mom," says Susie. "Bye, Sam and Curie, bye Timothy. Thank you guys for inviting me over, and I'm sorry for Jake. I hope he comes home very soon. I'll see you at school on Monday, Sam."

About an hour after Susie leaves, my father comes home. I haven't seen him look this worried since the crops caught fire. "What happened at the police station, Joe?" Mom says anxiously.

"Well, we filed the report for a missing person. They have people out right now looking for Jake. I told them his

description of what he was last seen wearing, what kind of car he drives, and his normal activities. They said the best thing we can do is wait." That's the thing about my dad. With something as serious as this, I know he wasn't just going to sit around. So, he searches the farm and the cornfield all the rest of the day, and spends all day Sunday looking for Jake, but still can't find anything.

Now it is Monday, and we still don't have any signs of Jake, but I still have to go to school. With Jake seemingly vanishing into thin air, my father wasn't going to take any chances. He decides to take Timothy to his school and drop me off at my school also. The day is looking really grim, but that isn't going to stop me from becoming a vegan. After I get done talking to Susie at lunch, I walk over to Gina sitting with her members of the ARAG.

"Hey, Gina, how are you doing?" I say.

"It's good to see you, Sam! Have you changed your mind about joining our group?"

"That's actually what I want to talk about. Something happened to me last Friday, and it made me change my mind about joining your group."

"Really, what changed your mind, Sam?" Gina says, eyes widening.

"Well, my friend was hurt – more like eaten – and she was my best friend, so I decided to dedicate my life to being a vegan."

"Oh, eaten," Gina stumbles to say. "Um, well, I'm glad you decided to join. There are five of us now including you, which would make six. So, there's me, the founder and leader, Jessy, Breanna, Mike, you, and Matt."

"Hey, guys!" I say with an embracing smile on my face. I then look down at Jessy's shoes. "I love your shoes, Jessy, 'they're really cute with the stars on them."

"Thank you, I made them myself," Jessy replies.

"Everybody is here now but Matt," says Gina.

"Did you say Matt?" I say.

"Yeah, Matt has been a part of our group since it was opened. Do you know him?"

Sam blushes. "Not personally, we have class together, and our family shares crops; I've seen him around."

"Well, you're gonna be seeing a lot more of him, because our group meets every day after school in the gymnasium. Sometimes at the park. Is that okay with you, Sam?" Gina says.

"Yes, but I probably won't be able to stay long, because my older brother has gone missing."

"I'm really sorry to hear that," Gina says. "Has your family or the police found anything?"

"No – nothing, no car, no shoes, shirt, nothing. He just vanished."

"Well, I hope that Jake turns up soon, and we all are very sorry."

"Thank you, Gina," I reply. "It's nice to meet all you guys, I better be going now. My fifth period class is on the other side of school."

"Okay, bye, Sam, see you soon!" the ARAG group says with smiles as wide as the sky.

"Ohh Sam, wait!" Gina screams. Our group is gonna take a camping trip this weekend, and I know your parents might feel away about the idea given all that's going on, but if you can we will be at the Golden Belt Park this Saturday."

"I'll ask my parents and let you know by Friday."

"Okay, awesome!" Gina replies.

I know that my parents will be horrified by the idea of me going camping with a bunch of friends at GB park, especially since my brother had been missing for over a week now, but Saturday is tomorrow. I figure this will be a nice time to try to spend alone with Matt. So, after dinner, I creep up to my parents' room to ask them about it.

"Mom, Dad, I know that things have been rough. Especially with the disappearance of my brother, Jake, but there's this group that I have joined at school."

My dad's face twitches and squirms as he blurts out, "What group?"

"It's called the A.R.G.A., and it's a group for young adults that are practicing veganism."

"Sam, this isn't because of what happened to the chicken, is it?" Joe says.

"Dad, that's exactly what this is. I said I was not going to eat another piece of meat for the rest of my life, and I meant it. This group is just for other people like me. It can help me cope and show me what it means to be a vegan." Joe looks at me with an unpleasant look.

"Now Sam, you don't know what kind of health risks being a vegan is going to have. I mean, you need meat and dairy to support you, honey, and just switching up your nutrition so quickly I'm not sure is the best choice for you."

"I know it won't be easy, Dad, but I also know it's possible. There are people who live healthy lives as vegans. That's why I'm joining this group."

"Joining the group! Me and your mother have to discuss this further."

"I think we already discussed it, Joe," my mother says. "Sam is a bright, very intelligent young woman. I'm sure she'll be fine with her decision. Isn't that right, Samantha?"

"Mom..."

"I'm sorry, sweetie, I mean Sam. Now, what is it that you wanted to ask your father and I?"

I'm really nervous now, seeing my father all twisted just by simply mentioning the group. I continue anyway. "The group is supposed to go camping Saturday night and I wanted to ask if I can go with them." 'Dad's chest grows tenfold. His skin becomes as red as the tomatoes he grows in the garden, which is saying something, because my father is of a darker skin color.

"Camping!" Dad yells. "Your brother is missing, and has been missing for a week now. Just vanished into broad daylight and you want to go camping at night with a bunch of friends you just met unsupervised?"

"No, Dad, we will be at Golden Belt Park, and there are several police shacks posted for miles. Honestly, the park is probably one of the safest places to be. Gina, the leader of the group, has already got her mom to approve the supervision from the police! All we need is permission from our parents!"

Dad takes a few deep breaths. "All right, all right, Sam!" Dad says, "But there's going to be a few rules, just for your safety." I nod in agreement. "I'm going to drop you off, and I want you to call me every hour on the hour. Your friend Susie has to come with you, and I will be there to pick you up Sunday morning, no exceptions."

My face lights up as I rush back up to my room, yelling, "Thank you thank you!" Straight to the phone I go to call

Gina and my friend Susie. My door slams shut.

Joe exhales very deeply. "What's wrong?" says Curie.

"We have one son that's missing, another son that doesn't talk, and a daughter that just flat-out decided to eat plants for the rest of her life."

Curie' gazes at Joe with a warm smile and a comforting stare. "We're raising children, Joe, nothing's going to be perfect. We just do the best we can do in raising them. The road can get bumpy sometimes. You know that, you ride them all day."

Joe smiles. "But sometimes you just gotta ride it out." Joe leans in to kiss her goodnight. "I swear that kid has the blood of the true heart."

"Not those stories again, Joe," Curie says.

"There are no stories, my mom was a special woman! The whole town thought she was crazy, but she wasn't crazy, Curie."

"I know, Joe," Curie says. "Your mom will always be special to me for birthing the man I fell madly in love with."

Joe grins at her. "Now let's get some sleep. We all have a busy day ahead of us."

Back in the room, Sam is busy making phone calls. "Come on, Susie, pick up, pick up!" Susie picks up the phone.

"Hello."

"Hey, Susie, I really need your help right now."

"Okay, you do know it's pretty late here, don't you?"

"Yeah, I know, but you know I joined the vegan group, and one of our first hangouts is to go camping!"

Susie pauses for a second. "Even with your brother still

missing?"

"Yeah, I know, but there isn't much we can do now but wait. In the meantime, we have to keep living. We're going to be camping at Golden Belt Park, and to let you know it will be secured. The only thing is my dad doesn't want me to go unless you come with me."

"Come with you!" Susie screams. "Bad enough you're actually joining those hippie, tree-hugging wool rats, and now you want me to come along with you to go camping?"

"Look, Susie, I know this is asking a lot of you on such short notice, but with everything going on I could really use a distraction and get my mind off of my brother going missing. Plus, Matt is actually a member of the group as well, and I think this might be a good time for us to actually get close to each other."

"Okay, fine," Susie says.

"Thank you, you're such a good friend. I've already talked to Gina, and they want us to meet them at the Golden Belt Fountain located at the center of Golden Belt Park by twelve tomorrow. If your mother can drop you off by eleven, we can make it there by 11.30, no later than 11.45. My dad is going to drop us off."

"Okay, Sam, well I guess I'll see you in the morning. Goodnight, Sam," Susie says, yawning."

"Good night, Susie!"

With a white beam of the morning sun blazing through my window, I awoke to hear strange voices speaking in the living room. I crept down the stairs just enough to see people talking without them seeing me.

There are two men in long, black trench coats, explaining to Sam's mother and father about the recent findings for the investigation in the disappearance of Jake. I listen.

"Excuse us, Joe and Curie, we're with the Central Intelligence Agency, better known as the CIA," the agent explains. "We have reasons to believe that your son's disappearance was part of a drug smuggling deal gone wrong."

"Excuse me, officer," Curie says.

"Agent," they both shout.

"I'm sorry, Agent," Curie says, mockingly. "I know ya'll are working hard to find my son, but there must be some kind of mistake. If our Jake was involved in any kind of drugs or smuggling, we'd be the first to know."

"That's right," says Joe. "My son is no angel, but he damn sure isn't a drug smuggler!"

The agents' facial expressions were the same as when they first walked in the door – vacant. As I listen to them go back and forth with my parents, I should have known something was off. Why is the CIA involved in my brother's case so quickly? All the things that they say seem like stuff that the local sheriff's department could have made the trip to tell us. It almost seems like we are a case study. They seem to already know what happened to my brother, as their questions begin to become more and more aloof. It went on like this for about thirty minutes before they decide to leave.

As they walk to their car, my friend Susie pulls in, so I quickly run downstairs to meet her at the front door. Susie walks to the front door as she waves to her mom goodbye.

"Hey Susie!" I say excitedly. "I'm so glad you came."

"Hey, Sam. I have to admit, I wasn't really feeling it last night, but I know this could be really fun. I mean, us underneath the starlight, campfire, a whole bunch of snacks, maybe scary stories and stuff. I'm not for all that other stuff you guys are going to be talking about, but I admit this could actually be really cool. By the way, who were those two creepy guys in the black trench coats?"

"Those two guys were with the CIA. They were talking to my parents about my brother's disappearance."

Susie gasps, "The CIA! Wow, Sam, this is huge, if the CIA is involved something big must be happening."

"I don't know, Susie, but they just gave me this really weird vibe. It's almost like they already knew what happened to my brother. Anyway, I think my dad is almost finished talking to my mom, so we should be heading out soon. Now are you sure you're up for this?" I say.

"Yeah, like I'll come all the way from the city just to turn back now."

My dad then walks out the door. "All right, are you girls ready?" Dad says as both of us are glimmering with joy, worked up and excited for this new adventure, now walking to my dad's truck and proceeding to get in. We drive off with country tunes playing. 'My mother and Timothy are standing on a porch, waving goodbye. Dad honks his horn as we waved back.

While Joe is taking the girls to Golden Belt Park for their camping experience, Curie is back home, still anxious and wishing that she had more answers than what was given to her. Timothy is in the living room watching his cartoons, and suddenly is interrupted by a breaking news banner. "We are sorry to interrupt your regularly scheduled programming. I am sure that most of you have heard about the disappearance of the young man, Jake, two weeks ago."

As soon as Curie hears Jake's name mentioned, she dashes from the kitchen to the living room. "We hate to inform you that there have been several more disappearances, victims seeming to vanish into thin air leaving the local authority scratching their heads and prompting the CIA to get involved. They say the disappearances are several drug deals gone bad, and that the criminals behind this are simply trying to make a point. Whatever it is, hopefully it's the last disappearance in our otherwise quiet little town. We'll have this and more coming up at nine."

The regular scheduled programming continues, and Timothy is once again zoned into the television. Curie goes back in the kitchen and begins to clean while keeping an eye on young Timothy. Meanwhile, Joe, Sam, and Susie are getting closer to Golden Belt Park.

"Look, Dad!" I say. "Golden Belt, five miles away!"

"That's right, Sam," Dad says. "We're almost there. Now, I want you girls to remember. I know you're going to be constantly watched by the police who are monitoring the area. I want you guys to remain vigilant. Look out for each other, and Sam please remember what I told you. I want you to call me every hour on the hour."

"Okay, Dad, I promise."

"That goes for you too, Susie. Stay in constant contact with your parents. You hear me, Susie? Susie!"

"Oh yes, sorry, Mr. Joe. I just thought I saw this strange red light in the sky for a second."

I laugh. "Yeah, do you not pay attention in science class. That's called the sun."

"Shut up, Sam, it wasn't that kind of red. It was, well, it's gone now, must be some new plane or something."

"All right, girls, here we are, Golden Belt Park." I have an awe-inspiring look on my face.
"Wow, Susie."
"Woah! Look at this place!"

Chapter 3

It's a Bird, It's a Plane, What Is That Thing?

Susie and I exit the truck, and are greeted by Golden Belt's finest. The officer starts to go over some rules and safety measures. I see the rest of the gang, Gina and Matt, Jessy, Breanna, and Mike. Joe, seeing that his daughter is in good hands, hugs and kisses me goodbye. He gets in his truck and rushes home to comfort his wife. Once the officer finishes their safety briefing, Susie and I are approached by Gina, the leader of A.R.A.G.

"Hey, guys! I'm so glad that you could make it. We have so many activities planned. Since the Sun is starting to set, who would like to go and get the firewood?" Matt quickly volunteers. "I will."

Susie rubs my shoulder. I hesitantly volunteers also. "Oh, I will, too!"

"Great," Gina replies. "Myself and the others will set up base camp."

"Sure, I guess," Susie replies with a slight smile. Matt and I begin to walk off and get firewood.

"You know, Sam," Matt says, "we've been so close to each other for a while but never really talked before."

"Damn, that's crazy," I reply.

"Don't 'damn that's crazy' me," Matt says, smirking. "Tell me more about Sam."

I try desperately to hide my blushing. "Okay, well, I'm a female."

"You don't say."

"No, true story."

"No, seriously."

"Well, as you know, my family owns a farm in which your family will be a co-owner of, an—"

Matt cuts her off. "I get that, but I wanna know some juicy stuff about you." I turn my head slightly away from Matt. "Hey, is that piece of wood over there good for the fire?" Matt smirks.

"Yeah that's actually perfect. We should head back now." Matt and I began to make their way back to the camp about fifteen minutes away, all while carrying the wood and dry leaves. I pasted my eyes back and forth.

"You okay?" says Matt.

"Yeah, I'm fine, I just don't wanna get lost..." I then whisper, "In your eyes."

"What?" Matt says.

"What? Umm... nothing. Hey, look, I can see the gang," I say.

"Looks like they already finished setting up the camp."

"Yeah, I think I can see it, it looks great!" says Matt.

"You know what's weird, though?" I tell Matt with a puzzled look on my face.

"Yeah, Sam?"

"While we were getting the wood and leaves, I could see the Ranger station from there, and I noticed that there weren't any officers in it, like, not one."

"You know, that is weird," says Matt, "I bet they're just out patrolling or getting lunch."

I shake my head in agreement. "Yeah, I think you're right."

As we both approach the site, I give my portion of the wood and leaves to Matt. "Why don't you go try to get the fire started, and I'm gonna see if my friend Susie is okay!" I walk over to her friend Susie, who is helping Gina prep snacks.

"Hey, Sam," Gina says. "Susie and I have all the vegan-friendly snacks ready for us to share stories here in a minute."

I begin to look around the camp. I look at the trees that are already starting to bloom. The constant stream of the river that is just beneath us. The sound of my friend Susie's warm laugh, and Matt – a seemingly perfect guy. Handsome, a farmer, and vegan.

Despite everything that's been happening, at that moment I feel peace. "Hey, Gina," I say, looking slightly startled. "Where are the others, Jessica, Mike and Breanna?"

"They also went out to find wood together just in case you guys didn't find any, but they should be back soon."

Susie is enjoying herself but is becoming hungry, and really trying to hold her composure as she blurts out, "Well, I'm not waiting, let's eat!"

Just as Matt starts the fire, Gina, Susie, Matt and I gather around the warm, cozy fire. Before grabbing her seat, Gina passes around the snacks that she and Susie had prepared just moments earlier.

"Okay, everybody, now we're gonna share our

moments of triumph from the things we've been through on our vegan journey," Gina says, *"There's a lot of pivotal moments that have led up to us making this decision. So, thank you guys!"*

"Sounds great, Gina, you're welcome," I say, including the rest of the group. *"Hey guys, wait, I'll be back,"* I say, remembering that I have to call my dad as it's been an hour already. I wander off a little distance to find a quiet place to talk to my dad. The gang starts to get into their stories as I starts calling him. I'm waiting for an answer, but the phone just keeps ringing and ringing.

Sensing nothing at the moment, I just try again and again, and I get nothing. I walk back over to my friends and speak to Susie. "Hey, Susie, my dad's not picking up the phone."

"So?"

"So, don't you think that's kinda strange? Especially since he was so adamant about me calling him."

"Maybe he was really tired and just fell asleep," Susie says.

"Yeah, I hope so. Anyway, I left a message for him." Gina goes on and continues with her stories when immediately several loud explosions go off, coming from the police department, one after the other, which seem to grow louder and louder. The gang rush to the edge of the cliff to get a better view of the police department. Looking over the cliff, we see nothing but devastation. No rangers on site, nothing but fire and lots of shrapnel everywhere.

We cannot believe this is happening, and we start to panic. I call my father again, but this time there isn't a dial tone. As the gang become more nervous, we decide to investigate the stations more closely. As we arrive at each station, there is no sight of any survivors. Each of the three stations spread within our camping district is like this. I think it would be best if we headed back to my place, since I live the closest. Scared there might be another explosion, we start running.

While in full sprint, Gina trips over something.

"Ahh!" screams Gina.

"Are you okay?" I say.

"Yeah, I'm fine. I tripped over this shoe."

"Wait, that's Jessy's shoe," I say, looking totally freaked out.

"Are you sure?" says Susie.

"Yes, It's the one with the stars on it. I remember complimenting her the first time I met her."

"What the heck is going on, man!" Matt yells. "How did Jessy's shoe end up here?"

"I don't know, Matt," I say, stammering, "but let's keep moving." A monotonous, shattering, slithering noise with a consistent growl visits the gang. One noise that seems to go on forever. We hide behind bushes and trees, petrified, patiently waiting for whatever's making that horrific noise to leave.

"Maybe it's just a bear," Matt whispers to me, as I'm hunched over next to him beside the bush.

"No, I don't think so," I whisper, "bears aren't really common at all in Kansas. Besides, whatever this thing is, it sounds like nothing I've heard before." Just then, the creepy growling sounds stop and the slithering halts.

"Okay, I think it's gone," says Matt. "Let's keep heading back to your place, Sam." The gang gather, coming

out of hiding to continue walking carefully and as quietly as we could, back to my house. Trying to avoid whatever that thing is that we had encountered.

We walk just like this for what seems like forever, until we are finally able to get back to the road. From there, I know it is a straight shot. "This is it," *I say,* "this is the street my father used to bring me and Susie to. All we have to do is follow it back."

"I'm gonna try to call my mom," *Gina says.* "There might be better reception here."

"Me too," *says Matt.*

"Agh, still nothing," *Gina says.* "How about you, Matt?"

"Nope, nothing." *So, we put our phones up and continue walking.*

Susie begins to moan. "Are you okay?" *I say.*

"Yeah, just a little tired." *So, the gang decide to take a break.* "Man, where is everyone?" *says Susie.* "I mean, there is not one person out here, and we've been walking for a while. We should have ran into someone by now. Where is everyone?"

I look to the moon and whisper, "Where are you Mom, where are you Dad?"

"We should keep going," *I say. After our short break, we keep walking and walking until we approach a riverbank that is not so welcoming, and smells even worse than it looks.*

"What happened here?" *says Matthew.* "It looks like a blood bomb went off." *The riverbank's water is bloody red, and thick like mud. The smell is almost unbearable; it's like something died and had been decaying for a while. There is also cotton-like thin strings, lots of them hanging from the tree, also dressed in blood.*

"I don't know if we should stay here," Gina says. "This place doesn't feel right."

"Doesn't feel right!" Susie screams in a panicky voice. "Look at this place! Nothing about this place is right."

"Shhh," I say, "guys, please calm down. Look in the river, something is making the water move."

"I don't see anything," says Matt, "it's probably a fi–"

Before Matt can finish saying the word fish, something shoots out the icky, bloody water, and stands before them. It is 7ft tall, and its skin is a thick and red scaly coat. It has no eyes, with a big, wide mouth, sharp teeth all around it, and long arms and multiple wide, slimy legs that look kin to squids. Matthew says to himself, "What is that thing?"

Susie screams at the top of her lungs, "Monster! RUN!"

Chapter 4

Monster?

They all quickly take off, freaking out at what they are seeing. The eerie, everlasting growl along with slithering noises begin again. It becomes louder as the creature gets closer to them. Gina, petrified at the thing, is frozen still, for the slithering monster doesn't bother her. It actually ignores her and goes straight for Susie.

"Ahhhh!" Susie screams as she runs into a nearby abandoned cabin, as the door had been left open. She quickly closes the door behind her and hides. She can hear the creature stalking the window, standing and wiggling. Eventually it leaves in a haste to pursue the sounds of Sam and Matt trying to get Gina to move.

"Come on, Gina, we have to go," Sam says, seeing the creature quickly heading straight towards them. Sam grabs Gina. She wants to head in the direction that Susie ran off to, but the creature darts at them from that way. Gina tightly grips on to Sam and Matt as they quickly make their way down to an area where the grass is just high enough to duck down and hide from the creature.

"Oh my gosh! Oh my gosh! Oh my gosh!" Gina says repeatedly.

"Shhh," Matt says, "it's coming." The creature swooshes over five feet from where they are hiding. It stands there, shaking and wiggling as if it was trying to sense them out. Suddenly, it stops shaking and starts to glow red. Almost simultaneously, a red glow in the sky starts to take form. The creature disappears as if it had faded from existence. The red glow in the sky goes away as well. "Did you guys see that?" Matt says. "That thing totally vanished into thin air."

Sam and Gina slowly rise up from the tall grass when Sam says, "I don't know what's going on, but we need to find Susie."

"Look!" Gina points out. "There's a flashing light coming from that cabin over there. That's the direction that Susie ran to. She may be trying to tell us to come." So, they quickly rush over as they are terrified that they might run into another one of those things. As they approach the cabin, they can see Susie flashing them down from the window. "Over here," Susie whispers. They all rush in.

Sam embraces Susie immediately, telling her, "I'm so glad you're okay."

"Yes, I'm okay," Susie replies, "what was that thing? Also, why did it only come for me?"

"I know, I noticed that, too," Matt says. "It went right past Gina as if she wasn't there."

"For good reason," Gina adds, "I was so scared I couldn't move."

"Maybe that's it," Sam says, "maybe the creature won't attack you if you're standing still."

Susie looks at Sam. "Yeah, I'm not sure I wanna test that theory.

"I was watching from the window," Susie continues to say, "and I saw it glow red. The sky glowed red also. I remember seeing that same glow in the sky."

"You did," says Sam.

"Yeah, when we were riding with your dad, coming to the park for our camping adventure."

"Some adventure," Matt cuts in to say.

Sam looks at Susie. "I- I remember you saying that. I'm sorry I didn't listen."

"It's okay, Sam."

Sam has a slight grin as she turns to everybody. "All right, we should keep heading back to my house and regroup. We need to figure out what these things are. We can see if our phones work there also, so you guys can contact your parents. I need to see if mine and my little brother Timothy are still okay."

She didn't realize it then, but she was demonstrating early signs of leadership, a quality that she had never possessed before. One that would soon be much needed.

The gang get back on the road they had originally been on. They walk and stay close to high grass and big trees, just in case they need to hide. Eventually, Sam's house can be seen from a distance. "There it is," Sam says. "I can see it from here. There's my dad's truck, too."

"Careful, Sam, there could be more of those things in there," says Susie. Approaching the house, they can see visible signs of struggle.

Joe's truck is still running with nothing but static playing on the radio. There is a long trace of blood from the house to where the truck had been left running. Sam, fearing for the worst, rushes to the house, leaving the gang behind.

She bursts through the door to find the struggle is indeed real.

There are things thrown all over the place. The same icky bloody waste that was found at the riverbank is the same all over the house. Trailing through the kitchen, back upstairs, and out the door. The others follow behind Sam not too long after she enters. They find Sam on both knees, clutching her mom's bloody apron.

As I sat there with my mind twisted and body still, in what I can only assume was my family's blood, I was still terrified of what these creatures were, where they came from, and what they wanted, but I knew what I wanted to do. I knew I wanted to make them pay. Pay for my mom, my dad, and my little brother Timothy. I had to assume my older brother was a victim of whatever these things were, too. It was hard to believe just a few hours ago I was camping. Possibly having a shot at a normal life. I was starting to feel normal.

A tear rushes down Sam's face, down her cheek, and hits the floor. Susie walks over to grab Sam's shoulder. She doesn't say anything, but she wants her to know she is there. The front door begins to shake and rattle. Everybody looks at the door with wide eyes, nervous and scared that those things have followed them. They decide to barricade the door with whatever they can find. The rattling from the door begins to shake more furiously. There is no doubt that something or someone is trying to get in. They see a really bright light. The shaking only continues for another brief second then, *boom!* Pieces of wood from the door go flying all over the place. The doorknob drops to the floor. They have been compromised. It is the two CIA agents.

"Quick, everybody hide, and don't say anything!" says one of the agents. They all scatter quickly to find a place to hide. Sure enough, one of the things is not too far behind them. It creeps up to the doorway patiently, waiting for the chance to find someone. Seeing that the place is already covered with bloody ooze, it leaves quickly. When the place is clear, they all begin to come back out.

"Hey!" Sam says, panting. "I remember you guys from the investigation of my brother and the other missing people in the town. What the haystack is going on here?" Sam says with a somber tone.

"We are not at liberty to disclose any information to the public," says one of the agents.

"The information you see is on a need-to-know basis," says the other.

Sam's face becomes red. "Look," she yells at the agent, "you guys lied about why people were being taken in this town. You had everybody living their perfect little lives knowing these things were out there, and now my mother, father and brothers are gone! So, you better tell me what I need to know, or I will go back outside and flag that thing down."

"Pff," the agent says, "and risk your friends being harmed?" The agents stare down Sam. Sam's friends all gather around her.

"You're testing my patients," says one of the agents. Sam makes a break for the door and is immediately grabbed by the fast-moving agent. "You're not going anywhere," he says, "but if you're in such a rush to die, fine, I'll tell you. It's not like I have much of a choice, anyway. Everybody's already been taken."

"Taken?" Matt says.

"Yes, taken, or rather abducted is a better way to phrase that."

"Abducted, like aliens?" says Gina.

"Correct. Their names are unknown, but we like to call them takers. The government has been tracking them for several decades with disappearances all over the world."

Sam's face scrunches up. "So, what have you done to stop this?"

"Not much we can do with their technology being so much more advanced than ours," the agent responds. "We have been able to keep them at bay with minimal abductions, but it seems that our greatest fear has come true. They have grown tired of a limited supply and have begun to take people more rapidly. Now it's even bigger than that; our sources tell me that this is being done all over the world right now as I speak."

"Where do they come from?" asks Sam.

"They are from an exoplanet just on the edge of the Goldilock system. As far as we know their main objective is to consume people."

"As in eating us?" says Susie.

"Yes, we, apparently for the better part of our existence, have been nothing more than an endless supply of food resources. In fact, our top scientists have speculated that we were implanted by them millions of years ago, so that when we reach our peak population, they will come to harvest. Peak harvest was achieved several hundred thousand years ago."

Gina shakes her head. "Yeah, but humans have only been on earth for about three hundred thousand years," Gina says.

"That's true," replies the agent. "The only thing is that

our top archeologist has discovered that there were humans here before us, whom they call 'blugah'. They think they are a far more superior culture than us. In fact, you can still see some of their greatest technological works, like the pyramids."

"What do those things have to do with technology?" says Matt.

"There are just old landmarks built by the slaves of ancient Egypt. That's what they want you to believe, and by 'they', I mean us," says the agent. "It actually is, or was, a very efficient renewable source of pure dark matter energy. They were able to power anything they built for food, shelter, travel, or weapons. The takers waited too long to harvest with the blugahand they advanced quickly. Unfortunately, they were not advanced enough. Fortunately for us, or we wouldn't be here. The fact that the pyramids are still around after all this time is testament to who they were."

"Wait," Gina says, "the takers – they seem to run right past me. It's like they didn't even notice me at all."

The agent turns his attention to Gina. "This is gonna be the key to our survival."

"What is?" Sam says.

"The aliens don't eat people who don't eat meat. It's something about their nutrition that craves people who eat meat. Eating a vegan simply won't sustain them, so they won't waste energy. However, in extreme hunger well, food is food. Once the food is contaminated over time from the waste, the 'aliens' leave, and the remaining will resort to cannibalism, thus becoming a target."

"Woah," says Susie. "That explains why it went straight for me, and straight past you, Gina. So, Jessica, Mike and Breanna must have been sneaking eating meat on the side."

"That is correct," says the agent. "It takes about two weeks for the trace of meat to leave your body fully. However, the moment you ingest meat, you will become a target for the process. So, I advise you guys to kick the habit quickly, bec– wait, you guys hear that?" the agent says in a frantic tone.

"Hear what?" says Sam. The agent begins to see several of the takers surrounding them. One by one, lurking in the shadows, they surround the entire home, covering the perimeter on every inch. "What are they doing just standing there?" says Sam to the agent.

"They are preparing to abduct us."

Susie reaches into her backpack. "Here, Gina, eat this piece of beef jerky."

"What, no!"

"You have no choice. We are surrounded, and if we are going to get abducted, at least we should be together."

"Susie's right," says the agent. "We know there is a mothership, but we are unable to pinpoint where it is. Maybe this would give us good intel on its location, and possibly how to bring it down. Their first plan is to disable all communication, and our defenses."

"That's true," says Sam. "I couldn't call my mom, and the ranger station was destroyed."

"Several defenses all over the world were severely impacted," says the agent. "We remained intact because of our current state of knowledge on the aliens. Oh no." The takers begin to glow red. "This is it, prepare yourselves."

Gina reluctantly scoffs down the bacon, gagging the whole time. Everybody gathers together, scared, and preparing for the absolute worst. They can see a red light in the sky just like when they encountered the takers before. The red light begins to illuminate the outer linings of their body. As the takers begin to disappear, the red, oozy, bloody mist starts to recover the already fully-covered things from Sam's once-beautiful, cozy home. There is a smell of death that is so repugnant.

Two by two they start to disappear. First, the two agents who draw their weapons out, preparing for a fight. They fade away into hope. Gina and Matt begin to disappear with Gina, holding her stomach, still nauseous. She then realizes that Matt is disappearing too, but how, unless he had been sneaking meat, too. Gina and Matt fade away into darkness. The last to go are Sam and Susie. They embrace each other in a tight hug, not sure if they'll ever see each other again. They both begin to shed tears.

Sam looks at a family photo, and remembers a time when they were all happy. A time when the possibility of terrifying, human-harvesting aliens was just in movies or video games. A time when her biggest concern was to have her crush find out that she likes him. When her brother disappeared, or when she ate her pet chicken. All these things that she remembers being a big pain in her heart. Not like this, though. This is a whole new world of agony, she thought. Sam and Susie take one more look at the glowing light above them, fading away into the process.

Chapter 5

Into Darkness

There they are, Gina and Matt, in a very cold, very dark room.

The room is so cold that they can barely breathe. Thankfully, they can breathe. Gina staggers up as she vomits the beef jerky to the floor. She takes one hard look at Matt. "How could you?" she says.

Matt has a shameful look in his eyes as he says, "I was never gonna be a vegan, I just wanted to be closer to you. I saw my opportunity to get close and I didn't want to pass that up. So, I pretended to be a vegan to know more about you, and maybe ask you out."

"Ask me out?" Gina says. "If you knew anything about me, you should know I don't like liars." Gina wants to tell him more about himself, but is interrupted by a crumbling sound. "Quick, turn the light from your phone on," Gina says. Matt, shaking from the coldness, flashes his light on. They are stunned at what they see. There must be hundreds of thousands of capsules, full of bodies. "Quick, Matt, over here," Gina signals. They gaze closer at one of the capsules. It was a woman, no more than twenty-four years old. She stands there in her capsule, frozen in time. Frozen, yet you can still see their eyes moving just a little bit. Their fingers twitch, and breathing was bradypnea. "This is horrible,"

Gina says. "It's so cold in here, Matt! We have to find a way out before we freeze to death or worse, maybe we could find the others, too."

With their cell phones not being able to pierce through the darkness much, Gina and Matt keep moving slowly down the eerie and still darkness that blankets them, alongside all the spine-chilling capsules that seem to never stop, with no signs of survivors in sight. "Wait," Gina says, "I hear something."

"Hear what?" Matt says, with fear and confusion muffling his voice.

The creature that Gina hears is a cubit. A nasty little creature that favors snakes, with little spikes all around it approximately one cubit long. The cubit's job is to constantly bite and roll its spikes around the body that's lying in the cryogenic state, piercing the skin and injecting the subject with antibodies. This gives them extra nutrients before going into the process.

Not being able to see them, the cubit wraps its spiky body around Matt's legs. "Help me, Gina! I can't move," Matt screams.

"Okay, but I can't see." So, she starts screaming and kicking violently in hopes that it will scare the creature away, but it seems to only attract more of them. The only warning is the sound of the spikes on the body of the snake-like cubit, scraping on the hard, cold floor. They can now hear many heading towards them, with Matt still trapped, barely able to move. He decides to make a desperate move and grabs the cubit with his hands, instantly piercing his flesh. He yells as he's pulling and pulling until the creature finally loosens its grip. Gina reaches out to him, gripping his bloody hand. With blood dripping behind them, Gina and Matt hide behind one of the capsules. The Cubit quickly goes back to providing nutrients for the bodies. Sensing a disturbance in the darkness, a couple of takers materialize from it. Trolling the area looking for the problem, twitching and slithering, they pass up Gina and Matt.

"That was close," says Matt. "I don't think I can be here for much longer. It's way too cold here and I'm losing too much blood."

"I know, Matt, I know," Gina says, exhausted, "but there doesn't seem to be any way out of here."

The taker's' glow begins to fade as the distance gets further away. Gina then rips a piece of her shirt off and wraps it around Matt's hands in an attempt to stop the bleeding. "Okay, now what?" says Matt.

"Now, we wait," Gina replies. "We can't see, and you're hurt Matt, Matt…"Gina whispers, "wake up, this is no place to die, we have to find a way outta here."

Gina sits looking around with frosty mist coming from her breath. She sees a glimpse of light in the distance. "Look over there, I see some light," says Gina. "I don't know if that's a better place, well, I'm sure it's not, but at least we can see."

Gina, holding Matt up, creeps towards the light, moving past capsule after capsule, hoping not to see another cubit or taker. As they move closer to the light, they notice that it is becoming harder to walk.

"What's happening?" says Matt. "It's like my foot weighs a ton."

"I don't know," replies Gina. "Mine is heavy too, but the light is getting bigger. Let's just keep moving as best as we can."

So, they keep moving towards the light, but the closer they get to it the harder it becomes to walk. They both are already exhausted, and Matt, being injured, just makes things more difficult. As if it isn't already difficult enough. It is about to get worse. The reason it is becoming harder to walk is because of the gravity in this part of the ship. It's heavier the closer they get to the light, or 'into process', a method to keep takers out before the process is finished. They can hear shrieks of screams and wailing moans coming from the light, which is a non-transparent, illuminated steel door, with no doorknob. Gina and Matt think tirelessly on how to get into the door, and away from the cubit and potential taker threats. The technology on the ship is too sophisticated for them to open the door.

"Open," Matt says.

"Really Matt?" Gina looks at him. "I don't think saying open will open it."

"Well, do you have any bright ideas?" Matt exclaims. "Besides, do we really want to go there? I mean, you hear all that screaming."

Gina looked down, scared. "No, I don't, but we can't stay here. It's too dark and too cold. We're gonna get in there. We have to find Sam and Susie. Gosh, I hope they're still alive."

Matt coughs. "Are you all right?" says Gina.

"Yeah, I'm just starting to feel tired again."

"I know you're feeling very tired, but you need to stay awake as long as you can."

"Hey, Gina, do you hear that?" Matt says.

"Hear what?"

"It sounds like someone is talking, but I can't understand what they're saying."

"Wait, I do hear it now, but I don't see or feel anything around me."

"Gina, look out!" Matt screams, panicking.

Something is lurking behind her, and takes a nasty swipe towards Gina. Luckily it misses, barely nipping her, as it gazes at Matt and quickly grabs him. Matt sits defensively at this humanoid creature's amazing strength. This humanoid creature is better known as a slider. It stands at 8ft tall, taller than a taker, but it is more intelligent and stronger, capable of speech and critical thinking. It is all black, and its body is more comparable to a human, all except for its elongated head that extends upward. It has sharp teeth, and a big hole in its chest, filled with quartz crystal-like material. The slider looks at Matt with its dark, cream-filled eyes and says something to him, but he can't understand the language. It strikes Matt with a deep slash across his chest. Gina goes running to one of the capsules to get as much attention as she can from the cubit, but because of the gravity in that part of the ship, she runs slowly. The cubit serpent-like creatures then immediately follow her, and begin to wrap themselves around Matt once they see his dangling body in the slider's grasp. Gina had hoped that the cubit would distract the slider so they could hide.

"Matt," she screams, "I'm so sorry."

"It's okay, Gina," Matt struggles to say, suffering from dyspnea.

The hungry and anxious slider's middle chest starts to light up blue. Matt feels the heat as the charge in the slider's chest gets brighter. Gina looks desperate as the slider is almost finished charging its blast. She runs toward it to try to free him. Matt, taking one last look at Gina, grabs a cubit and shoves it into the chest of the slider. The charge into the slider's chest and it overloads and explodes, instantly disintegrating the slider and Matt. The explosion disables the transparent door, and Gina was sent flying from the blast unconscious, into process.

Chapter 6

Into Process

I remember when I awoke that day, or night – it's hard to determine what time of day it was on the ship. I awoke to a blinding white light that covered all surroundings like a milky void. I was starting to think that I had died and was at the gates of heaven, but when the light dimmed down, I started to see very unheavenly horrors that were happening around me. The first thing I couldn't help but notice was the smell. It was like back on Earth at the riverbank, but so much worse. What I saw next shook me to the core, and was the reason behind the madness of the fetid smell. As far as the eye could see there were columns upon columns of people that had already been captured. They were brought in by capsules from another part of the ship, which I now know to be into darkness. What the agents were saying was true. I wasn't sure what was happening in the dark room, but once they came from there to here, they would be placed onto this table that stood upright. From there, the things I saw would forever turn my stomach.

It was true, really true, that they were harvesting people. Once on the table, they would rip their body apart, limb by limb. Each limb was skinned, and the blood was drained. Each organ was snatched, and their eyes were removed. No part of the body was wasted. So many people, so many screams; they treated us like animals.

My friend Susie lay on the floor, still unconscious. I began to think about the other people on Earth that were vegans. I knew that the aliens didn't take them, but with all that blood and gunk spewing into the atmosphere, it was only a matter of time before vegetation was tainted. Most importantly was that my parents and brothers were still alive. I wanted to find them as quickly as I could.

"Wake up, Susie." Susie moans and awakes to a blurry sight of Sam.

"O-M-GOSH! Sam, are we still alive?" says Susie.

"Yeah, but do we wanna be? Look around you." Susie looks around at the horror show.

"I can't believe this is happening to us," says Susie.

Sam takes a deep breath. "I know this is, well, I don't know what this is, but I know we need to find our friends. Let's get moving before something comes." Sam and Susie continue to move along, hiding at every corner carefully to avoid anything that might be watching them. They even manage to avoid a few takers. "I don't know if I could watch this anymore, look at all these people," says Susie. "There are kids, families, and even babies. I just don't want to look at this anymore."

"I know, but we have to keep moving," replies Sam. So that's what they do, looking for any sign of life that isnt alien or being processed. *The excruciating pain these people must be in,* Sam thinks to herself. Then, she immediately stops dead, frozen in her tracks.

"What's wrong, Sam, why did you stop?" Susie looks at Sam as Sam looks still at what is her greatest fear coming true. It is her parents, Joe and Curie, strung up, waiting to be processed. Curie is completely unconscious, and Joe is still conscious but barely cognitive. The machine begins to process Curie. Sam screams, "No, Mom!" She frantically looks for a way to stop the machine. "Quick, help me find something to stop this, Susie!" They both look for a way to stop the machine, but the machine is already ripping her unconscious mother apart. Sam felt a deep hopelessness, in that all she could to stand there in watch her mother limbs being ripped, skinned, and drained one by one. Sam's face grows pale as she watches her mother being slaughtered like a pig on an assembly line.

She doesn't know what to feel, she just feels empty. She feels angry, as she stands there in shock. Susie, still completely terrified that something is lurking, comes over to comfort Sam.

"Hey, Sam, I'm so sorry about Curie, but I think we should get going. I'm getting a really funny feeling that something is watching us. This place is really creeping me out. To your mom, I'm really sorry."

Susie's eyes become watery as she starts to think about her parents. If they are even still alive. Sam stands there and tries to put herself together. She hears a muffled voice coming from where her mom once was. "Sam," the muffled voice says. "Sam." It was her father. She runs over to get as close to him as she possibly can to hear him. "B... b... bl-" Sam's father tries desperately to get the words out.

"What is it, Dad?" Sam yells with tears falling down her face. She watches that once-strong and bold, humble farmer struggle to gather words. It is the hardest thing Sam has had to watch, trying desperately to understand her father. He is fighting, going in and out of consciousness. Joe knows that he isn't gonna have much time. So, he gathers all the strength that he can to say one last thing. "Blood of the last true heart, my mother."

Sam looks confused, as she has no idea what that means. "Dad, what does that mean?" *Blood of the last true heart.*

Joe looks Sam in the eye and says, "Your blood."

The machines start up and Joe is about to be processed.

"Wait, wait! Dad, please, I have to find a way to make this stop!"

Sam looks around, but then Susie grabs her. "Look, he's tryna say something."

Joe, now being lifted into the air, muffles off these last words. "Your, blood, true, blood." Then he begins to be processed. Sam has already seen what happened to her mother, and can't bear to watch what is about to happen to her dad.

The screams that her father cries out, however, she will never forget. She has never heard her father in so much pain. Unluckily for everybody, the process was inhumane, as they took the head last. This leaves the host alive for most of the process. That is, the ones that are not unconscious. Sam and Susie have to watch and smell most of it. The screaming from her father soon stops as the process is nearly over, and he had now been decapitated, but the scream from Sam is the bloodiest shriek you will have ever heard. Sam's eyes begin to glow purple, a mixture of red and blue.

"Sam, your eyes," Susie says, "they're glowing purple!" Her eyes soon fade back to their natural color. "Are you okay, Sam?" says Susie.

"Yeah, I mean no, I mean, I don't know," replies Sam. "I felt this energy all over my body, and my mind felt like one."

"Like one?" Susie says, confused.

"Yes, like one, I don't know how to explain it."

"That's okay," Susie says. "It looks like we won't have much time. Something dropped in here." The thing that dropped in is a slider. The slider stands there, gazing at Sam, and Sam right back at it. This lasts for a minute until the slider rushes over to grab Sam, striking Susie down to the ground. The slider looks at her, and he finally says these words with a groggy voice. "True blood." The look on Sam's face is unimaginable. It's what her dad had been talking about, but why is this thing talking like this? Why is it talking at all? It knows about true blood. Whatever true blood is. Sam then kicks the beast and is able to break free from the grips of the slider. Sam and Susie, now back on her feet, begin to run away. Sam takes one more last look at where her father is before stumbling forward.

It is nearly impossible for a human to outrun a slider. With the enhanced ability of the slider's anatomy, the slider will be more than hot on their trail. Sam and Susie are dumbfounded, as they don't know who this new creature is. They are afraid that they will have to deal with takers, and that the takers are the worst thing they will have to encounter, but here is this new creature that had caught up to Sam and Susie as they run into the darkness. The slider corners the girls and begins to speak. "True blood, you have returned."

Sam looks beside herself. "True blood, I don't know

what you're talking about, but I do know that you're gonna pay for my family's death. You're gonna pay for what your kind has been doing on this planet for generations. I'll kill you all!"

Susie looks at Sam, frightened that Sam is making the slider madder. The slider begins to salivate.

"Homosapien, you are no more than tonight's main course." The alien growls and murmurs. "You won't stop us. No one can stop the Primes. Not you or any true blood before you."

The slider lets out a death-defying scream, alerting all nearby takers. The slider looks at Sam. "You see, we always win. We feed and we win." Takers begin to emerge and gather around Sam and Susie.

"We need to think of something fast, Sam, or we're gonna be finished."

The takers begin to get ready to do what their natural breed does, and that's take. Susie, looking very anxious and scared, begins to scream, but Sam stands there in this newfound courage. She was just waiting for the takers or sliders to make a move. The takers react and charge Sam and Susie. Sam doesn't hesitate to put Susie behind her to protect her. Thinking that this is the end, Susie begins to say her goodbyes, being that they are outnumbered by these creatures that are aggressively charging to eat them. The slider with a mundane grin on its face stands back and waits for its meal to be served. The takers stood next to Sam and Susie begin to cover them with their ooze that illuminates their body. It becomes very hard to move. The takers put on a slightly stronger ooze than the one that seduced the abductions from Earth.

"Take these two into the darkness, I want them plump and nourished immediately,"says the slider. The takers take them closer and closer to the darkness. Sam and Suzy notice they are becoming extremely cold and approaching a non-transparent illuminating door. The takers are about to gain access to the door.

Everything is quiet, then a powerful explosion shatter's the transparent door. The explosion wounds and distracts the takers, and knocks Sam and Susie unconscious. They wake a few seconds later with high-pitched ringing in their ears. Sam stumbles to her feet. She takes a second to look around and notices Gina's unconscious body lying on the floor. Susie follows shortly behind. They try to wake her by yelling her name, but she won't wake up, and the right side of her face had been burnt badly. The slider, having become very impatient, begins to charge his beam that's going to send one devastating blast to what he now perceives as a threat.

With Gina unconscious and Sam and Suzy still woozy, things begin to look grim, and all they can do is watch as the slider beam is now fully charged. The slider does not hesitate to release his beam. The girls feel the heat as the beam gets closer and closer. It is just about to hit when a portal opens, and out runs a strange, slightly blue male. He uses the shield to reflect the beam.

"Into the portal, please!" the strange male yells at the girls. Sam and Susie then grab Gina's body and quickly rush into the portal. They are able to escape into hope.

Chapter 7

Into Hope

Sam and Susie step through the portal holding Gina's body. The place they arrive at is called Into Hope. It is an oasis, such a beautiful place; a small sanctuary full of humans living in peace, much like the humans on Earth but more, and slightly blue, hidden in a secret sector of the ship from every foul creature on board. They are greeted by the blue male that saved them.

"Welcome to hope. We are your ancient ancestors. My name is Bluepopolis, or Blu for short. Your friend is badly wounded."

"Yes, she was hurt in the explosion," says Susie.

"Understood," says Blu, "we have a place where she could heal and rest. I will have some of my men take her there." Blu sends some of his men to get Gina and take her to the place of healing.

"At last, Sam," says Blu, "we've been watching and waiting for you."

"For me?"

"Yes, we have been waiting for someone who has true blood. Hopefully the blood of the last true heart. To finally put an end to this genocide of megaannum. Has your father ever mentioned anything about true blood?"

Sam looks down. "Yes, right before he was processed,

he mentioned it. Everyone is gone, my whole family. I have no one left." Blu gives a concerning look of empathy.

"I'm sorry for what happened to your family. I, too, have suffered great loss. Please, Sam and Susie, sit. I will tell you the story of true blood. It started shortly after my people were harvested. Plugging 90% of our population, leaving only 10% so that we would not go extinct. So that we can repopulate and prepare for the next harvest. Besides the slider, takers, and cubits you've seen before, there's another threat, a much more powerful one. They're called the Primes."

"I've heard of them," says Sam, "a slider we encountered on the ship was talking about how they would never be defeated."

"That slider is correct. There are three Primes. They are very ancient beings believed to be at least a googolplex of age. Their energy is drawn from dark matter itself. They're always engulfed in it and there's way too much of it. The only thing that can kill a prime is a prime, or someone of true blood. They are responsible for the out growing growth of life in this universe. You see, what the universe gives, it also takes. Knowing all of this, one of the primes begins to feel regretful and remorseful. During the repopulation phase of my people's harvest, he fell and mated with a woman. In this desperate attempt, he was hoping to spawn a warrior with the blood of a prime so that they'll be able to help kill the other two primes who would not change their ways.

"That was a great plan in theory, but the other primes have managed to sneak out and kill every true blood since then. The primes operate in synergy. So, it wasn't long before they could sniff out the prime hybrids. As for the prime who set this all in motion, no one has seen him since. We were only able to survive on this ship thanks to the minor dark matter manipulation that we learned on Earth by a being that we now know to be the prime that spawned true blood. We now call this Prime, Prime X. The last true blood was your grandmother, your father's mother."

"My grandmother, I never knew her. She was dead before I was born, and my father never really talked about her."

"That's because it was widely believed that she killed herself. The town at the time thought she required psychiatric help. She claimed to see strange glowing big men that weren't there, and that she was glowing purple. Of course, we know those to be the Primes. The purple glowing, I know you are already familiar with."

Sam nods her head. "My face was glowing purple when I confronted the slider."

"Yeah, and it was glowing blue at her home one night," says Susie.

"There are several colors on the spectrum of true blood," says Blu. "There is black as an overwhelming nature of death and hate. Green is becoming one with the Earth, and nature. Yellow is powered by fear. Orange is a heightened sense of positive emotion. Red is an overwhelming sense of anger and power."

Susie gasps, "The takers glow red, and the sliders' aura was black."

"Yes, these creatures were born of anger and hate. The blue glow that you see is for overwhelming sadness or a sense of grief. Purple is the awakening of the spirit, most accurately related to our fight or flight system. The purple you saw that night is fight or flight, a lighter purple. The awakening of the spirit is much darker. It comes with reasoning and understanding of the spirit. Then there's the white. It's the fullness of the spirit. This is the glow of the primes."

"Then I could glow white too, eventually," says Sam.

Blu looks at Sam. "That's what we hope for."

Sam takes a deep breath in, and a deep breath out. She looks at Susie, then at Blu. "I have to stop them, not just for my family, but for everyone's family. Blu, could you help me control true blood? So that I could glow white!"

"It doesn't work like that; it's about synergy, your emotions, and the universe," says Blu. "When it's time to glow white, you will."

Susie smacks her teeth. "Well, I hope the time is sooner rather than later."

Sam had begun to think to herself about what she could do. Something that could help her come to perfect synergy with her emotions and the universe.

"Is there something to eat here?" Susie says.

"Yes," replies Blu. "Next to the place of healing there is a hut for vegetables. Please help yourself."

Susie smiles. "I never thought that I'd ever be happy to hear that." As Susie walks to the hut, Gina is walking out of the place of healing. Susie and Sam run over.

"It's so good to see you guys alive," says Gina.

"You too," replies Sam and Susie. Sam looks at the burnt scar on Gina's face left by the blast.

"Aren't I beautiful?" Gina says, smirking at Sam.

"I'm sorry, I didn't mean to stare. Does it hurt?" says

Susie.

"No, I don't feel a thing, only this mark to remind me."

"Didn't you and Matt get beamed up together?" says Sam.

"Yes, Matt, er, he sacrificed himself to help me escape. He didn't survive the blast. I'm sorry, Sam, I know how much you liked him." Sam's body began to turn red for a second. Blu and the others took a step back. Then Sam began to calm down. "It's okay," Sam says. "He died protecting you, so he died fighting, which is exactly what we are going to do! We won't let his death be in vain. Not him, my mom, my dad, my brothers, your families, or all the other generations of people on Earth!" They started to gather around when Sam made her speech.

"This has been going on for far too long! The Primes want to come in and take whatever they want whenever they want, because they think no one could stop them. Well, I will, but I can't do this alone." The eyes of the broken spirits begin to rise. "I know y'all brought me here for an obvious reason, and I won't let you down. Now, let's go take our planet back."

"Woo! Woo! Woo!" the ancient humans yell.

"We are still missing some people," Sam says. "Blu, have you seen two guys in long, black coats?"

"No, we tampered with the algorithm of the mothership's beam that abducted you. It was supposed to bring you right here. In order to do that we had to go back to parts of the ship that's unsafe. Which is everywhere but here. Somebody went back in and tampered with it further which split you and your friends into different sections of the ship. I wrote the code that disrupted the beam. This, of course, allowed me to look into it, and I did not see the two men that you speak of."

"That's because we didn't want you to see us," a mysterious voice says from a distance as if it were coming from the sky. Everyone looks around frantically to suddenly see the two agents standing before them. "There you guys are," says Sam, "you made us worried."

"You should be," says the agents.

"I don't understand," Sam says, confused.

"The rudimentary obtuse mind never does." Sam and her friends look even more confused. That's when the agent's clothes began to fade away, and their bodies begin to glow a scintillating bright white. Blu and all the ancients begin to cower as if they had seen this before. In fact, they had seen this before. They are the ones they feared the most, they are the Primes.

Chapter 8

The Fall

At a moment's notice, the whole place becomes tense. You can feel the fear in the air as the Primes stand there, unperturbed. Nobody has a clue what to do or how the Primes found them. The one thing they know for sure is to fear the worst. A prime presence means death is soon to follow as Blu looks very worried.

"They found our spot, and Sam isn't ready," he says. One of the primes begin to laugh menacingly.

"Your spot," he says. "You have no spot here or otherwise other than the belly of the beast. We knew ever since the disappearance of our brother that he was helping you animals hide on our ship, but we could never find you. That is until your precious savior arrived. Isn't that right, Sam? We will always be able to track the use of our energy, especially in our ship."

"You don't know anything about me," Sam screams.

"Oh, but we know you quite well. The uncertainty and insecurity that you feel about yourself. That you don't trust anybody, and you are so uncertain with yourself that you'd rather make friends with a cockerel. I'm sure he felt congeniality swirling around in your stomach juices."

"Shut up."

"Such a shame, I prefer my meat, well, human. Oh, and

then your poor crush, Matt. My takers had such fun licking him off the floor."

Sam is becoming agitated at the harsh words that the primes are spewing, but she knows that she needs to stay calm and not show her glow. Sam is fully aware that the primes know what level of glow she is on. She doesn't want to antagonize them in any way. Blu has a contingency plan just in case the primes ever find their location. Prime X releases some of his energy to create an exothermic reaction, or a bomb that will stun the Primes long enough for them to escape. The only problem is that somebody has to be within three feet of the Primes.

"Sam, can you hear me?" Blu says.

"Yes," replies Sam, "but why are you in my head?"

"We are able to stimulate the neurons in your brain to create a pathway. We can then communicate without speaking. Ordinarily, the human race should have achieved this a century ago, but humanity's senses have been dulled to the use of radio waves."

"Aren't radio waves non-ionizing?" says Sam.

"Yes, however, the waves affect the neurogenesis process shortly after birth. Your senses are heightened by the blood of the primes, so I'm able to communicate with you directly."

Sam nods her head in agreement. "Wouldn't the primes be able to hear us?"

Blu's face remains constant. "Yes. normally, but since they're busy monologuing it doesn't seem like they know what we're doing."

"Okay, great," replies Sam, "so what's the plan?"

"There's an old technique that could work that would

allow us to stun the primes long enough to escape back to earth. I have two portals left. I used one to help you and your friends escape earlier. This next portal would take everyone who passes through back to the farm. There we will regroup."

Sam looks confused. "But what is this technique I will use?"

"You will have to channel your anger or red glow. This could possibly allow you not to be hurt in case of a direct attack from a Prime, but, honestly, I'm just not sure your red glow could handle an attack from beings that strong."

"Well, we're gonna find out."

Blu smirks. "We are gonna need a distraction if you're gonna get that close."

Sam looks worried. "But won't they kill you?"

Blu sighs. "Some things are worth dying for. Of all true bloods, I have never seen one quite as woke as you, and it's been a long time. Speaking of time, we don't know how long it's been down on Earth. It could be a couple hours, weeks, or years that have passed. Time works differently on this ship thanks to the dark matter the Primes consume. Though if not for that, we would have been dead millennia ago, but when it's time I will signal for you." Sam again nods her head in agreement.

While the primes are busy implanting fear into the minds of the ancients, one by one they pass the bomb through each other's hands until it is gripped tightly in Sam's hands. Susie looks at Sam as if she knows, and wants to wish her good luck. The primes then focus back on Sam. "Do not be fooled," they say, "whatever you're planning will never work. You shouldn't worry about us; you should worry about your new friend. In fact, Gina didn't tell you about Matt's crush on her."

Gina looks at Sam. "I was gonna tell you eventually," Gina says. "I just only found out myself right before he, well, you know."

"HAHAHA," the Primes laugh. "You see, you can't even be loved right. You will never be able to control the blood of the Primes. No matter how much you care about your precious family which are no longer here."

Sam begins to grind her teeth.

"Maybe if you were more aware of the immediate threat instead of crushes that don't even like you, you would have felt our presence. I wish I could say that your parents' deaths were special. They weren't, they were just a couple out of many deaths. Likely a snack for my takers. You probably don't need me to explain that part to you. You saw it yourself."

"Enough!" Sam screams. "You're right, I should have been more aware, but not of you. Of the love that surrounded my life all this time. How loving and understanding my parents were. The shenanigans my older brother taught me, and all the things I wanted to teach my little brother timothy."

Sam begins to glow purple from her head to her toe. "All that love I had, and you took that away from me!"

The Primes smirk. "Love! Love is just a chemical we compounded to get you animals to breed."

Sam's face gets intense, and the glow heightens. "Then you have created your own destruction! To love only what happens, what was destined. No greater harmony," she says.

The primes and Sam are now quiet, gazing at each

other's energy. Sam charges with the purple glow of the awakening spirit, directly at the Prime who looks unbothered.

"NO!" screams Blu. Sam, knowing that the Primes would be too confident, stops inches from them. She opens her palm. The Primes are shocked to see what is in her hand, but before they can react, the energy of the bomb releases upon them. An intensely high magnitude of energy. They are stuck in time. Blu quickly opens a portal to Earth, giving him only one portal left. "Everybody in the portal, now!" Blu yells. "We don't have much time." So, everyone does just that; all the ancients, Gina, and Susie.

"Come on, Sam, this place is caving in." Sam rushes over to the portal, taking one last glance at the Primes, who look beyond pissed off."

"Nowhere to run," the Primes say, frozen still. This sends an eerie chill down Sam's spine as she hops through the portal, back to Earth.

Chapter 9

Home Sweet Home?

A portal opens to what used to be Sam's parents' farm. Although now very unrecognizable, Blu's hypothesis is correct. It has been sixteen years since Sam and her friends have been on Earth, but to Sam and her friends it only feels like sixteen days. To the ancients, it has been centuries since their feet touched soil. Thanks to the alien pollution and bad maintenance, the soil is badly degraded to the point of desertification. The livestock that were left roaming the night of the abduction have now been reduced to bone.

"Egh, is everybody okay?" says Blu.

"Yes, I'm fine," Sam says, standing with her fist balled as her purple glow begins to fade. She turns to Susie and Gina. "Are you guys all right?"

"Yes, we're fine," Gina says.

Susie, looking exhausted and down on one knee, says, "Speak for yourself! Feels like my head's going to explode."

"Allow me to explain that," says Blu. "Prime X was able to directly manipulate dark matter particles and what they called deity wave particles. Deity wave particles are particles that exist outside of time, hence deity. This allows them to temporarily alter time using the portals. It must have been powerful to make, because he only gave me three, and now I have one left. To conclude, direct stimulation through these portals for ordinary humans is why you feel like this. Not to worry, it shouldn't last too long."

"I hope not, but we need to make our way to somewhere safe," Susie says, lying on the floor, still in pain from the portal.

Gina looks at Sam. "She's right. We need to find some food and cover." Sam stares at the barren graveyard that used to be her home. Scattered in the wind are the bones and dust. The sky's dark red now, with clouds like blood clots. Almost all the rivers and streams that were once a crisp pristine blue, now run a dark, bloody red. "Blu, how long will it take the Primes to come looking for us?"

"I don't know, Sam, they could very much be on their way now. More than likely they're gonna send takers, or sliders to fetch us."

Sam takes a deep breath. "Well, at least that would give us some time to get ready for when we see them again. Blu, gather everybody up quickly. There's a Big EZ mart that is a couple blocks away. I'm sure we could find some preservatives and shelter there for the time being."

"All right, everyone, let's move out," says Blu.

Blu, Sam, Susie, and the rest of the ancients set off for The Big EZ.

Sam, Susie and Gina are still trying to make sense of the gap in time. Tired and afraid, they arrive at the Big EZ mart as the sun is starting to set. Sam looks to the group. "All right, guys, this is it. We need to grab any food well-preserved. Dry cereal, peanut butter, canned goods, and any medical supplies you find. The vegans were left behind, so this whole place could have been ransacked by now. We are looking at a sixteen-year gap, so there might not be much of anything."

Sam, Susie, and Gina go looking for food, and since the ancients are well trained in healing medicine and using natural herbs, they go to scout the area for such things. Exploring this newfound world isn't easy for Sam and her friends. They had only a brief moment of survival skills camping before everything went south. Still, there is very little room for shakiness. This doesn't stop them. They are all busy searching every little crate they can, making sure to scavenge even the smallest things. "Do y'all you see anything?" says Sam.

"No, I haven't found anything yet," says Gina. A loud clash of pans falls to the floor. In the darkest corner of the store, followed by an eerie squeaking wheel of a shopping cart rolling nearby.

"Guys, what was that?" says Susie.

"Is there anyone here?" says Sam.

Susie looks into the dark corner. "Yeah, it's not a good time to play hide and seek."

"I'm not." A shaky voice begins to speak, coming from the shadows. It is a man. He has abrasions all over his body, and is malnourished. Gina walks over to him. "Are you all right, sir?"

"No, it's my daughter. She is stuck inside of a deep hole out back and is too young to get out, I-I'm too weak to save her, I can barely move. We barely find food as it is, and anything we do find is only enough for my daughter. I'm too weak to save her. Please, can you help her before those things come back, please!"

"Of course we will," says Sam. "Where is the hole that your daughter is in?" The man's eyes shift to the left, signaling the back door. "Okay, we'll get her, don't worry, we will get your daughter back. Then we can help you find food together."

Sam, Susie and Gina creep to the back door. Sam opens the squeaking door to see a huge hole in the ground at least twelve feet deep. "Hello, little girl, are you down there?" Sam says. "We're here to help! Don't be scared, your dad sent us to get you out." The girls hear nothing as their voices echo back to them. Gina, standing behind Sam and Susie, peeks over their shoulders.

"Maybe we should..." Sam looks back at Gina,

"Maybe we should what?" A line of blood runs down Gina's mouth and drips from her chin.

"Gina!" Sam screams. Gina's body then falls to the ground to reveal the man with the squeaky voice. The same man that had asked them to help his daughter.

"Oh my gosh, Gina, no!" says Susie.

Sam looks at the man. "There was never anyone to save, was there?"

The man smirks, "I think you know the answer to that."

"Murderer," Sam yells at the man.

"Murderer? No, I'm hungry, and your little friend is ripe for the stabbing," he says, laughing frantically. Sam's body begins to glow red. "Hey, your body is glowing like th-th-th- those things!" the man says, frightened, so he panics and kicks Sam in the stomach, forcing her to fall into the hole. She hits her head on a rock as she lands on the ground.

"Noooo, Sam!" Susie screams, backing up as the man

approaches her with the knife.

"Guess who's going in the hole. Guess who's going in the hole," the man says, taunting Susie. Frightened, backing up, she slips and falls into the hole. She lands on her ankle, twisting it. The man laughs even more frantically. "Yes, yes, yes, yes, now I can save you two and eat her first. I can stretch this meal out for at least a month. Oh, if I were you, I wouldn't scream, or they'll eat you first." The man grabs Gina and drags her back through the door, into the store.

Susie holds her ankle. "Sam, please, wake up."

Chapter 10

Red Baron

"Wake up," a misty voice echoes from the ceiling as Sam wakes up in her bed. "Good morning, Samantha." A soothing voice washes over her like warm water in a shower.

"Ma-Mom, you're alive! How?"

"Of course I am, sweetie, why wouldn't I be?"

Sam begins to cry as she rushes over to give her mom a big hug. "Everyone was dead, you, Dad, Jake, and Timothy! These aliens came and were abducting people, they were using them for food, Mom, they captured and harvested everyone. There were these ancient aliens called the Primes! We escaped their ship with the help of some ancient humans, and came back to Earth! Nothing was the same when we came back, everything was all messed up."

"Sounds like you had a nightmare," Sam's mother, Curie, says calmly. "You worked yourself up into quite a spell, haven't you? You were so tired and worked up after what happened to your chicken last night, you just went to bed. Your dad drove Susie back home." Sam looks disoriented and confused, but pleased.

"So, it was all just a dream."

"Thankfully so with everything you just told me," Curie says with a smile on her face. "You see, your brother Jake is outside, talking to his girlfriend.

"What about Timothy?"

"He's in the same place he was hours ago, on the couch, watching cartoons in the living room."

Sam looks at her mom. "You don't know how happy I am to see you. It just felt so real. I can't-I can't believe it was just a dream." Sam's mother touches her on the shoulder, comforting her.

Moments later, as Sam is finishing her breakfast, she hears a rumbling in the driveway. It's Sam's dad's truck pulling into the driveway. Sam rushes from the dinner table to greet her father at the door. When she opens the door, she finds no one there. Just the truck running.

Jake and his girlfriend are also gone. Sam slams the door and runs back into the kitchen to find her mom nowhere. Timothy has disappeared, also. Sam starts to sweat as she calls her mother. She then hears a large thump on the ceiling, coming from upstairs. "Mom?" she says with a cracked, high-pitched voice. Sam starts to walk up the stairs, slowly and cautiously. Step by step, the thumping becomes louder and more violent. She approaches her bedroom and cracks open the door. She sees a horrifying image of her mom with glowing red eyes. The thumping was her mom, convulsing on the floor. Sam rushes to turn on the light switch but it doesn't turn on. Her mom lets out a loud shriek which turns Sam white with fear.

She immediately turns around and runs back down to the living room. There, she finds her two brothers and father doing the same thing her mother was doing, convulsing on the floor violently. She doesn't know what to do, so she curls up into a ball in the middle of the stairwell, wishing that whatever was going on would go away. Then, a glow begins to occur. This time it is black. The aura is all over her body, just like the purple and red glow before. The only difference is that this one feels heavy. Like it is hard to hold onto her shoulders. The violent thumping from upstairs stops, and the same in the living room. The bodies of her brothers and father stand up, floating a foot off the ground with their heads dangling down, lifeless for a few moments. She then hears a light moan coming from her father. He raises his head and begins to open his eyes. "Sam?" her father says, clearing his throat.

Water immediately comes to her eyes. "Dad, is that you?"

"Yes, it is me."

Sam runs to give him a hug so tight. "The last thing I remember was being on a ship looking down at you." Joe's head leans down with tears dripping from his face profusely.

"I'm sorry you had to see that, Sam."

"No, Dad, I'm sorry you had to go through that. I tried so hard, but I didn't know what to do. I-I couldn't cut it off!"

"That's okay, Sam, there's nothing you could have done."

The look on Sam's face of hopelessness that she couldn't save her father is heartbreaking. "Dad," Sam says, curiously, "what is true blood?" Sam had already heard the story from Blu, but she wants to hear what her father has to say about it.

Joe drops to the ground and walks to the window. "I really wanted to tell you sooner about this!" Sam waits patiently to listen to her father. "It has been so long since the last true blood, my mother, your grandma. My grandma used to tell me all these stories when I was a little boy. I thought they were just stories until it happened."

"What happened, Dad?"

"They killed her, my mom. Everyone thought she killed herself, but she was murdered. My mom loved me, and she would never do that. I know she would never do that. All the stories my grandma used to tell me made sense once I got a little older. She was killed by a Prime."

"Yes, Blu told me all about them."

"Who's Blu?" Joe says.

"He's one of the survivors from the last major harvest."

"Sounds like you've been around, Sam."

Sam chuckles. "Yeah."

"How long has it been since the harvest?"

"It's been sixteen years, Dad."

"Wow, sixteen years, but why are they still here, and you don't look a day older than when I last saw you!"

"It's the Primes, Dad, something about the dark matter in the ship that makes time work differently, I don't really quite understand it yet."

Joe levitates, gliding closer to Sam. "I'm not sure what you know already, but you don't have much time left, so let me tell you what your grandma told me," Joe says.

"What do you mean, I don't have much time left, Dad?"

"Well, right now you are in the black glow. There are eight glows, and each one, except for the white, is based on emotional connection with oneself; the purpose of the glow. Only when you are in white glow will you be able to manipulate these glows without purpose."

"Right, but how will I know when the time is right for

white glow?"

"My mother used to say that only true blood will know."

"Sam, wake up." The echo again!

"Wait, Dad, that sounds like Susie!"

"That's because you're sleeping, Sam. The Black glow is focused on death! Meaning you could bring back spirits of loved ones during times of meditation or sleep. It looks like you're starting to wake up now."

"How can you tell, Dad?"

"I'm starting to fade away."

"Dad, wait, I have so many more questions! I don't want you to go, Dad, please stay!"

"I wish I could, Sam. Just remember who you're fighting for, what you're fighting for. They took everything, but they cannot take our love for each other. Even in death, I still love you! You have the power over your mind, not outside events. Realize this and you will find strength. I love you, Sam."

Joe immediately fades away as Sam is starting to wake up.

"Dad, please wait, I love you too."

With Joe gone, the foundation of the dream begins to crumble as the black glow around her body fades. More determined than ever by her father's words, the glow turns dark purple. *I won't let you down, Dad, I promise.*

The voice rings again. "Sam, Sam!"

Chapter 11

The Awakening

Sam's body begins to glow in the outside world.

"Sam, wake up, please!"

Sam, with blurry vision, looks up at Susie.

"Well it's about damn time! Are you okay? You fell and hit your head on this rock."

"Yeah, I'm fine, how long was I out?"

"For at least twenty minutes."

"That's it? Wow, it felt like hours!"

"Ahhhh!" Gina screams in agonizing pain.

"Come on, Susie, we have to get out of this hole," says Sam desperately.

Susie grunts as she stands to her feet. "I'll try, but I can barely stand. I broke my leg when I fell down here."

"Stand back," Sam says, "I wanna try something." Susie stands back as Sam walks toward the dirt and places her hand on it.

"Okay, now what?" says Susie.

"Just wait until I can feel it."

"Feel what?"

Sam's body starts to glow green. Susie watches, as the green glow is very beautiful to see. Roots shoot out from the ground, creating a ladder to get out of the hole. Another weaker root emerges from the ground that Sam breaks to place against Susie's ankle to help support her.

"Somebody, please help!" Gina's loud cry comes from inside the store. Sam grabs a hold of Susie to get up the stairs as fast as they could. Sam barges through the door to find Gina strapped to the table. The crazed man has a machete, sharpening it in preparation to skin Gina. The crazed man is shocked to see Sam and Susie.

"What, how did you get out of that hole? Why are you glowing green? Not that it matters, because you're too late." The crazed man pulls back a sheet that was hiding Gina's dismembered leg.

"Oh no, Gina, we're too late!" Sam says as she hangs her head in disappointment.

"Damn right you're too late! She's already lost too much blood to ever recover from this, and with all that yelling, the takers are soon to show. So why don't you let me finish my meal, and I'll let you two go!"

"You tricked us into saving a daughter you don't even have!" Sam says as she starts to approach the crazed man. "You then trapped us in a hole and threatened to eat us! Now, one of my friends is going to die and you want us to bargain for our lives? No! I think you misunderstood this situation; today, you die." Sam stands there and stares the man down as her aura begins to turn red.

The crazed man notices the same aura as the takers. That same glow she displayed right before he kicked her into the hole. Only this time there is no hole. Seeing the fire in her eyes, the man panics, grabbing the piece of raw flesh from Gina's leg, and begins to run away.

"Stay here, Susie," Sam says as she follows the man, gaining on him as the red glow commands it. The man finally trips over what seems to be nothing, and is back in a corner as Sam slowly approaches. The crazed man then begins to beg for his life.

"You expect me to show mercy, as if you didn't just give us an ultimatum, live or die? You tricked us, and tried to eat us, and now because of you my friend Gina is badly hurt, and is probably going to die. No, today you die too!"

Sam's body was already glowing red, but now something new is happening. Now her eyes are glowing red as well. It is like Sam isn't there anymore. Her emotions are becoming too high, at this point and she is losing control. The man begins yelling more fiercely than ever. "Please don't kill me, I'll do whatever you want!" Sam walks up to him and phases through his body slowly. While she walks through his body, his vital organs begin to come out with her. His heart, lungs, kidneys, liver, and spleen fall to the floor. The man stands there for about five seconds, as his body is in shock, before collapsing to the floor.

Susie looks at her friend cautiously. "Are you still with me, Sam?" Susie gets no reply. Sam suddenly focuses her attention on Susie. She starts to approach her just like she did the crazed man.

"Sam. I'm your best friend, remember that we need to stop the Primes." Sam continues to approach her. Scared for her life, Susie begins to cry.

"Please, Sam, I can't do this without you."

Sam freezes in her tracks and her glow begins to fade away. "I'm so sorry, Susie, I just have gotten so tired of losing people, and I couldn't control the rage."

"It's okay. We've been through so much already. It's really hard not to feel that way."

They hear a 'please help', followed by a cough and subtle moan in the corner. Sam and Susie run over to the table where Gina is laying. Her body is dismembered and pale.

"Gina, we didn't make it in time," says Sam.

Gina gathers all the strength she has to make one last statement. She turns to Sam and Susie and smiles. "Look at us, how did we end up here? This doesn't feel real, but it's okay. Look at me, look at my face, I stood no chance." Gina starts coughing. "You guys have to stop this thing. Stop the whole damn world if you have to, but don't let them take anything else from us. No matter what, I-I, I will always treasure our time. I will always…"

Gina stops with a glossy look in her eye – she has lost too much blood. Sam, and Susie both stand with tears rolling down their cheeks, saddened at the loss of another friend. They grab her body and wrap it in sheets, gently placing her in a small ditch of four feet.

They are suddenly disturbed by a loud mighty bang that lights up the sky white as it strikes the ground.

"Oh no, Blu."

Chapter 12

Last of a Dying Breed

The sky's a dark red now, with clouds like blood clots. Almost all the rivers and streams that were once a crisp pristine blue, now run a dark, bloody red. The world wasn't always like this. Sometimes it's hard to remember how things used to be. Everything happened so fast that I barely know what's going on at times. With the loss of my family and friends, I just need to remain strong and keep fighting. Fight, fight for the ones that can no longer fight for themselves. To change this everlasting calamitous event.

Susie and Sam rush to see what the loud noise was. Fearing the worst for their newfound companion Blu, they run as fast as they can.

"That doesn't sound too good, Sam," says Susie. The ground is still trembling from the impact. Sam and Susie come to the corner of the loud noise as they peek around it, only to find yet another horrible horror scene. Looking at the mess that had been made, it might have been better to be back on the ship. Sam knows it is only a matter of time before the Primes catch up to them.

She didn't expect them to find her so soon. They must have been pretty upset about the energy bomb released on them. They look around and they can see all the remaining ancients on the ground, dead, most of them dismembered from the impact of, yes, the Primes landing. Every last ancient is dead except for one; Blu. "Come from around that corner, thief!" say the Primes. Sam and Susie walk from around the corner as the Primes ask. "Do you like what you see? These pests should have been eliminated a long time ago. Our brother has only delayed the inevitable. When we find him, he will be stripped from existence. Oh, look, I have a present for you!"

The Primes pick up Blu from the ground. "Blu!" Sam and Susie scream.

"True blood, you're still alive," Blu murmurs, coughing up blood.

The primes slam Blu's body back on the ground. "Silence, you pathetic anachronism! The Great Harvest is at hand, and we are behind schedule. This nuisance of 'a true blood is some hero savior' stops here today with you. You're no true blood, you're a thief of power. I should have you chained to a mountain to die every day with your liver being eaten by an eagle. This is Kansas, however, so I'll be perfectly fine grinding you and your friend to dust and spreading your ashes across the Milky Way."

Sam has an eager look on her face, but she is also terrified. "The only thing I'm grinding right now is my teeth," Sam says. "You know for someone so powerful you sure do talk a lot. I think that I've heard enough of this garbage."

"Yeah," Susie adds. "If you're all-knowing and powerful then why are we still alive?"

The Primes have a dead stare on their face as the energy of them and Sam is still. The Primes do not know that Sam has crossed the black glow yet, and is more in tune with her power. The Primes start to glow an intense white as they speak to Susie. "You know what, Susie? You're right, there's no reason you should be alive at all," say the Primes.

In a split second, the Primes release a wave of energy directly towards Susie. It immediately engulfs Susie in flames as she falls to the ground, suffering fourth degree burns. "Susie, oh my god, Susie, no!" Sam yells as if she feels the fire herself. It is an absolute shock to Sam, as she didn't even see the attack coming. She kneels by her side until she stops breathing. The Primes stand there, laughing mockingly at Sam.

"Wow, some big hero, you just can't keep no one alive, no one's alive. Everyone around you is dead! You have no family, no friends. It's a pity you still carry on. Let's make a deal, give up now and I might kill you as fast as we possibly can, filthy abomination."

Sam staggers to her feet, physically and emotionally wounded. "You're right. Everybody is dead, everybody but you." The red glow bursts around her, releasing a devastatingly large amount of energy towards the Primes.

"Rage," say the Primes, unbothered, "is all you have learned displayed. My poor child, let me show you." The Primes are instantly behind her with a magnificent white glow. They grab her head and charge a blast right to her face, knocking her back to her friend Susie who lay there with her eyes open, dead, looking at Sam. "Maybe you should take some advice from her," the Primes say, taunting Sam. "Get up, we're not through with you. Let's try something more dramatic." They pick her up and throw her all the way back to where Gina is buried.

"Oh, I remember this one, too bad my takers didn't have a chance to eat her first," the Primes say, chucking her back to the place of the ancients' last stand.

Sam is beginning to worry more than she already had been. The Primes are just too fast, and too strong for her to handle. Without Blu around to teach her the white glow, she is never gonna be a match.

"Without your white glow, you're never gonna be a match! Besides, your so-called sensei is down for the count, but you still wanna fight! Still! I can feel it. You're optimistic about death, good, I will show mercy with a quick, painful death." The Prime's charge a huge blast for Sam's quick death. While they do that, Sam hears a quiet whisper in her head.

"Sam, can you hear me?" It is Blu, communicating to her using telepathy, just like before.

"Blu, you're still alive!" Sam says. "Yes, I can hear you, and I'm sorry about your people." An eerie sadness comes over Sam. "Susie and Gina are both dead, and I don't think I can stop the Primes."

"You can't. I'm going to send you somewhere using my last portal. Maybe he can help you."

"He? He who?" Sam says in confusion.

"No time to explain, this line of sub consciousness is very sensitive. When you get there just wait, and he will find you. I wish we had more time to train. I wholeheartedly never expected to live. Make no doubt about it, Sam, you are the one. You proved that simply by being able to awaken the flow of energy. We just need a little more time, and a little more help. That which I will provide for you using the portal."

"Blu," says Sam, "if the Primes see you using that portal to help me escape yet again, they'll kill you for sure."

Blu starts to laugh subconsciously, which echoes through Sam's mind. "I'm already dying," he says. "The Primes must be stopped, and you're the furthest I've ever got, you're the best shot humanity has! Some things are worth dying for."

A darkness lingers in the minds of Blu and Sam.

"No, just dying." A third mysterious voice echoes through both Sam and Blu's minds. It is, of course, the Primes. They've been eavesdropping on them since the beginning of the conversation. "Another portal," the Primes say, "is your big plan? Even if you are able to release it in time, that would only be delaying your very overdue extinction. I will find you, but you're never gonna reach that portal, because you're already dead." The Primes snap their fingers, and Blu's body bursts completely open, leaving nothing but blood and organs.

"Blu!" Sam screams, defenseless to stop them as she can barely get off the floor.

"Oh no, so much for that plan!" The Primes mock Sam as they stand there towering over her. They are about to strike a fatal blow of energy to Sam when a mirror-like bright circle appears around Sam. It is the last portal of Blu. He was able to put small amounts of the energy of this last portal to transport anyone the portal energy was attached to upon his last heartbeat. The portal is to transport them to a specific location, originally designed as a failsafe for the ancients in case he died, to protect them from becoming extinct. It would send them to an undetectable place. The ancients unfortunately died before Blu, releasing the energy back to the portal. Blu then sends the energy to find Sam as she buries her friend Gina. The portal quickly swallows Sam as if she had entered a blackhole. The primes yell out in fury that she has escaped again!

Sam wakes up in a white, empty void with no one in sight.

"Hello," she says. Suddenly, a figure of a man starts to approach her. "Hello, who are you?"

The man says nothing and continues to walk closer.

"Blu said you'll be able to help me."

The man finally is within five feet of Sam as she looks up at him. The man extends his hand to help her up. "Long time no see, Samantha," the man says.

Sam looks confused. "How do you know my name?"

The man smirks and says, "What's the matter, Sam, don't you recognize your own brother?"

Sam's eyes widen. "Timothy?"